Elena and Family

HakJin Kim

창조와 지식

Elena and Family

HakJin Kim

Characters

- Elena Lee
- Henry Lee (father)
- Eva (mother)
- Evan Lee (younger brother)
- Grace Lee (grandmother, Henry's mother)
- Julie Lee (Henry's stepsister)

- Lily Kim
- Nora Yoo (Lily's mother)

- Mike Hong
- Alex Hong (father)
- Sunny Hong (mother)
- Ron Hong (younger brother)

- Ms. Kim (the manager of the nursing home)

Elena Lee, a mid-teen, trudges across the pavement to the nearest bus stop. Behind her, a three story building adorned with private academy signs is bathed in the warm summer evening light. As she reaches the bus stop, she checks her bus arrival time shown on the digital display board and stands in line behind a few high school students. She glances at them since they are her classmates in school and a private academy as well, but neither of them says hi to her keeping their eyes glued to their cell phones. After a little thought, Elena turns around and steps out of the line to walk home.

The day is still bright though it is seven o'clock in the evening. It seems to be good enough to walk. While walking down the sidewalk, Elena intentionally looks at each of the trees which are lined up along the street. It is nothing new because she passes the trees on the bus ride home, but she gets sentimental especially these days due to her uncomfortable circumstances. She takes deep breaths feeling a gentle breeze blowing against her face. The smell from the trees seems to get her to calm down. Soon, her emotions are jumbled when thinking about what has happened in the past few days.

Elena definitely knows that something is happening to herself at home, let alone in school. It started a week ago when she found out that Eva made a flight reservation to Canada for herself only. It was odd because Elena was always accompanied by Eva, her mother, to spend summer vacations in Canada where Evan, her younger brother, is a junior high school student. Moreover, it was a big surprise when she found that Eva got a year off from her work to stay there for about a year. Before then, there was no secret between Eva and Elena, so it was hurtful to know that Eva kept it quiet and didn't tell her. What is even stranger was that Eva who had been a loving mother began to be cold to Elena, which made it hard to communicate between them.

Elena lets out a sigh and suddenly, thinks of Lily who she hasn't seen for months since Lily goes to an international high school. They had always been together until they parted ways. Without Lily in school, Elena feels pathetic because no one speaks to her in school and even in the private academy. Once in a while she tries to figure out why any of her classmates hasn't spoken to her from the beginning of the first year of high school. Still, she doesn't have any clear answer, guessing that she is just not likable.

Then, Elena feels a hand on her shoulder. She stops and turns her head to see who touched her.

"Oh, Lily. What a surprise! I've been thinking about you. What brings you here?"

"I stopped by the bakery on an errand for my mom. And I saw you pass by. What makes you look so serious? Are you in trouble?"

"No. I was just walking home," Elena says.

"How are things at your school these days?"

"You know, without you,... How have you been?" Elena says.

Elena looks delighted to see Lily.

"How about you?" Elena asks.

"Not bad. But there is a thing that is worrisome to me," Lily says.

"What is it?"

"I wanna get into college here in Korea, but I should go to U.S. college because of my mom. She is stubborn." Lily says with a sigh.

"That's why your mom put you in that school, so you can't refuse her wish," Elena says.

"Did you talk about it with your dad?" Elena asks.

"No, not yet. Didn't I tell you that? My parents divorced last year."

"What? Is it true? I can't believe it."

"Yeah. My dad had another woman. I was shocked at first, but soon accepted it cuz it could happen. Now I understand he can love another woman." Lily shrugs her shoulders.

"Yeah, I guess so," Elena says.

Then they just keep walking in silence. Elena who is tall and slender with fair skin looks plain next to Lily who stands out among the crowd.

After walking for some time, they reach a condo complex two blocks before Elena's place. Lily stops and says to Elena, "Now I live here. We moved to this area this spring. How about having dinner at my place?"

"Oh, okay. I'd love to." Elena says with a smile.

Soon, Lily calls her mother to ask whether she can bring Elena. At that moment Elena sees a familiar car passing the gate. She waves her hand to stop the car because it is her father's. Elena goes near the car and the driver's side window rolls down.

"Oh, Elena. How come you're here?" Henry says with his eyes wide open.

"Dad, you're not supposed to be here, huh?" Elena says.

"I have to meet someone who has business with me. Is your mom home?"

"How do I know?" Elena shrugs.

"I should go. See you home." Henry drives away after hearing the horn honking behind him.

Elena turns around as she hears Lily calling, and they get to Lily's place.

Lily opens the door to let Elena in and, to her surprise, her mom is there.

"Mom, are you leaving now?"

"Yes, Sweetie. Oh, hi, Elena. How are you doing?"

"I'm good, thanks! How about you, Ms. Yoo?"

"Doing great!"

"Girls, order pizza or burgers for dinner," Nora says.

As soon as Nora closes the door behind, Lily says,

"Sit down, Elena, it's our time without mom!"

With two glasses of milk, Lily sits next to Elena and shows some pictures of her which were taken with her high school friends. Elena looks through each of them and point to a man.

"Who is this guy?"

"Mike. Do you think he looks good?"

"So-so. He just looks familiar. Is he our neighbor?"

"No, but he lives in a single-family home just a 10-minute drive from here. He came from California last year 'cause his dad was transferred to Seoul."

"I see. You already have many friends," Elena says.

"Yeah, how about you?"

"Oh, you know, I don't think my classmates care about me. So…"

"Elena, don't say that. You're smart and nice, so you'll have good friends sooner or later," Lily says, smiling.

"Well... I hope so. Anyway, did you join any school activity?"

"Yes, tennis. Did you?"

"No, not yet. But, you know, I'm not sure I'll have any spare time to do sports. I need to study to get into a good college," Elena says plainly.

"Yeah, right." Lily agrees.

Elena looks at Lily who seems excited and, suddenly, feels tears welling up in her eyes. She tries to hold back her tears, but Lily doesn't miss it.

"Elena, what's going on? Did I hurt you?"

"No, but..." Elena says calmly.

"To be honest with you, I'm feeling sad these days. It's because of my mom."

"Really? Why? She always checked up on you when my mom didn't do it." Lily says with a doubtful look.

Elena fixes her gaze on Lily and tells about her current circumstances. Lily nods to show she is on Elena's side, but thinks that Elena overreacts to her mother.

"Well, you have to talk to Eva about what you feel," Lily says.

"Yeah, but she never gave me time to speak. She just walked away whenever I tried to go near her. It felt like she didn't want to see my face," Elena says.

Lily looks at Elena in the eyes and says, "Yeah, now I get it.

Something must have happened to her. I can't imagine what it is. What if she is having an affair with someone?"

Elena looks at Lily with surprise.

"What? It can't be!" Elena says loudly.

"I'm kidding! But my mom is seeing someone." Lily winks at her.

The food Lily ordered has arrived.

"Elena, let's have pizza."

"Okay! Eva doesn't care how late I come home. She even doesn't know whether I sleep in my bed or not." Elena shrugs her shoulders.

"Oh... But you have me!"

"Yeah, but you have lovely mom who supports you with heart," Elena says with a sad smile.

"Come on! Elena, I'm sure you have good parents. Don't misunderstand your mom, please."

"Oh, I've got an idea. What about having a boyfriend?"

Lily says after biting a slice of a pepperoni pizza.

"What? Who then?"

"Mike. He is very nice. He is fun, you know," Lily says.

"Well, we will see," Elena says.

After they finish the whole pizza, Lily takes out her iPad.

"I have an assignment to do. Elena, as long as you're here, can you help me with my math project?"

"Sure thing."

Then, they are engaged in solving math problems.

"Wow. You're the math teacher's daughter," Lily seems excited.

"Oh yeah?" Elena smiles and says, "By the way, it's already 9 PM. I lost track of time! I've gotta go. Lily, you made me feel much better. Thanks."

"Alright! Let's hang soon."

It isn't dark yet when Elena is outside to go home. After a few steps, she looks up at the sky and sees a half moon. She takes a deep breath to refresh herself and begins to walk fast under the dim street lights. There is no one around, but she doesn't feel afraid to walk alone at night. As she is near home, she feels like the home doesn't belong to her anymore.

Elena steps inside, but no one is home yet. After tossing her backpack onto the coffee table, she lies down on the sofa and thinks of Lily who brought laughter to her. In a minute, she rises to her feet when her phone is buzzing on the table. She takes the call.

"Hi, Dad"

"Hi, I'll be home late."

"Okay, Dad, you'd better text mom." Elena sourly says.

Actually, Elena doesn't care whether Henry comes home late or not because he always keeps himself busy by running a company. Elena only cares about Eva who used to ask about her whereabouts.

Elena goes to bed early feeling exhausted but she keeps tossing and turning in bed, her mind full of thoughts about the situation she is in. Eva has become distant from her, and it makes her feel small at home. About an hour later, Elena hears the front door open and Henry's steps coming toward her room.

"Elena, I'm home." Henry calls out.

He cracks her room door open when there is no response. At that moment Eva comes home.

"Elena is in a deep sleep, I guess," Henry says to Eva.

While Elena stays in bed without making noise, there is silence in the living room. A little while later, Eva says, "Henry, I have something to tell you. Come to my room."

"We can talk here."

"Okay, then. First of all, I wanna say that we've had a happy life even after we had to adopt Elena, your niece. But my happiness is shattered when I found out you've had an affair with a woman."

"What? I didn't cheat on you," Henry says.

"You're a liar, Henry. Be honest with me."

Elena springs up in bed and begins to eavesdrop at the door with bated breath.

"Henry, I pretended there was nothing wrong between us 'cause I was afraid of the consequences if I disclosed your affair. But I realized that the chances of your coming back were slim. Your lover is your high school sweetheart, right?"

Henry doesn't answer her question.

"In this situation, I don't know what to say. At first, I was gonna separate from you to think about our future, but I've changed my mind. I want a divorce."

While listening to Eva, Elena's heart begins to race with nervousness. Now Elena finds that Henry is her uncle related by blood and Eva is just his wife.

Eva continues to talk to Henry.

"We've cared about each other after having dated for a decade and married, and still I want you back. But I know you won't be the same anymore. So, I took a leave of absence and prepared to go abroad to live for a while. And at this point Elena weighed on my mind, but I'm not gonna take her with me. I want Evan only, our own son, not an adopted daughter."

"Oh, Eva, don't say like that. Elena is our daughter. You've loved her," Henry says with a sigh.

"Not any more. She's just your niece. And I feel like you don't care about Evan," Eva says, staring at him.

Henry also stares at Eva and says without blinking his eyes, "What makes you say so? I love both of them."

"Eva, you need to have a break for a while and I would join you in Canada sometime later."

"What do you mean? Are you planning to live in Canada or just come visit us for a few days?"

"Well, I don't know." Henry glances at the door of Elena's room.

Henry seems worried that Elena might overhear them.

At last, Elena flops down on the floor leaning against the door. She can hardly believe what she heard. Soon afterwards, Elena climbs into bed and lies flat on her back.

Elena mumbles, "Oh my God! Now I get it. Henry cheated on Eva.

Eva has changed and become cold to me because I am his niece. That's why she hasn't even looked at me."

With a rough breath, Elena tries to recall everything about her childhood. She knew that she was their beloved girl and there was no sign of an adopted girl since she was treated well along with Evan. All of a sudden, she feels like she is having a nightmare and at the same time, she wonders why her birth parents let Henry adopt her. When that thought hits her, she is about to dash out the door to ask Henry right away what happened in the past, but instead, she just bursts into tears, hiding under the blanket. She feels so sad, thinking that she has no parents anymore, only an uncle, and Eva has turned against her because of Henry's affair. She is also sorry for the truth that Eva is an adoptive mother.

Elena doesn't know what to do in this situation which is too much for a sixteen-year-old girl to bear alone. Elena feels that the night is too long to spend, but she falls asleep fast due to fatigue from the shocking truth.

The next morning, Elena wakes up earlier than usual and slips out of the condo with some extra cash. It is still dark before the dawn. While walking down the street, she thinks of Lily who would stay in bed enjoying her Saturday. She texts, "Hi, I'm leaving home now. Are you free today?"

Elena just wants to talk with Lily, who knows what she feels about

Eva. In a minute, Elena gets the message back from Lily.

"This early? Well, but I have a tennis lesson this morning. How about this afternoon?" Lily texts.

"Are you sure you are free this afternoon? Then I'll wait."

Elena heads to a cafe which is open around the clock. She sees the sun rising over condo complexes. The buildings and the road being bathed by sunlight seem different to her at this moment. She feels deserted because she now finds out that Henry and Eva have the only son, Evan, and besides, Eva will cut ties with Elena and Henry soon. She shakes her head because she can't accept this reality.

Elena enters the cafe, where there are a few people who are mostly college students. She sits at the far end of the hall with a glass of milk, and she texts Lily where she is now. While sipping milk, she stares blankly outside. Once she knows that she was adopted as a baby and never met her birth parents, she can't help but wonder who they are, let alone why they have forsaken her. She wants to ask Henry about that, but she is afraid how her life will change after getting the answer for that. In a couple of minutes, she recalls the day Henry showed the picture of her grandmother. Since Elena has got a glimpse of the photo at that time, she doesn't remember her face but knows that her grandmother was put into a nursing home a long time ago because she had dementia. Elena has no information about where her grandmother was put to stay, and so nothing brings the name of the nusing home to mind. Elena starts to do a search online for an elderly care facility to find her grandmother who must have known about the past years. Elena keeps on doing it, regretting that she didn't hear Henry out. She racks her brain and finally remembers that it begins with 'Love' and the full name of the nursing home comes to mind along with her grandmother's name--Grace--which might have been mentioned once but erased in her head. And as a next step, she has to know the way how to get to the nursing home, 'Love and Care'.

Elena sits back after she completed the first action for the process to find her birth parents. As long as she knows she was adopted by her maternal uncle, she can't be the same as she was before, and there is a question as to why Henry has been quiet about the adoption. He could tell Elena about the reason his sister consigned Elena to him. And now Elena realizes that she doesn't take after Henry who has square jaw and high cheekbones with dark skin, which she has never thought about that before.

Elena closes her eyes and imagines about how her birth parents look like. At that moment she feels the vibration of the phone and reads the message that Lily is coming now.

Elena sees Lily walking inside the cafe with a teenage boy following behind her. He looks like Mike, but Elena can't be sure it is him.

"Hey, Lily, you always look gorgeous!"

"Yeah? Thanks." Lily smiles at Elena.

"Elena, this is Mike. The tennis class was canceled, so here we are. Mind if he is with us?"

"No. Hi, Mike." Elena says with a calm voice and Mike says hi.

"What's up? Leaving home meant you're getting away from home?"

"Yes and no. Well... I don't know if I can talk about it in front of Mike."

"Yes, you can. Mike has a lot of experience because he lived in different countries, right?"

"Yeah." Mike smiles at Elena.

"What is it? Did Eva hurt you?" Lily asks.

"No. Oh, Lily, guess what? They are not my parents." Elena lets out a sigh.

"What? Who are they?"

"Henry is my maternal uncle. Eva is his wife."

"Really? I can't believe it. How did you know it? Did Henry tell you?" Lily says with startled eyes.

"I overheard it. Lily, what am I suppose to do?"

"Well, I don't know what to say. But you're not a stranger to Henry, so ..."

"You mean, I'd better stay home. By the way, Eva wants a divorce because Henry's having an affair with another woman," Elena says.

"Oh my gosh! That's why Eva's been cold toward you," Lily says.

"Yeah, she felt betrayed and became distant from me at the same time cuz I'm his niece," Elena says with a serious look.

"But, Elena, you have to stay home. They're still your parents," Lily says, shrugging her shoulder with her palms facing up.

"Maybe you're right. But I wanna know the reason why Henry took me in. He should let me know what happened to his sister, my birth mom."

Mike cuts into their conversation and says to Elena, "I agree with you. As long as you're his niece, he should tell you about your birth parents. But I think there went something wrong, so that's why he should be quiet about it. Hmm..."

"Anyway, Eva has turned into a cold fish. By the way, does Eva have any relatives in Canada except Evan?" Lily asks.

"Yes, she has two sisters. That's why she sent Evan to study there," Elena answers.

"When is she gonna leave you and Henry?" Lily asks again.

"I have no idea. But she'll file for divorce before she flies to Canada," Elena says.

"Oh, then, she's gonna demand alimony a lot in compensation for emotional stress caused by his affair," Mike says.

"Oh, you're smart! You know a lot." Elena says.

"Elena, his dad is a company lawyer. So, you can ask Mike whatever you wanna know. How does that sound?"

"It sounds okay!" Mike says with a smile.

And then Mike stands up to order some sandwiches for lunch.

"Girls, I buy you lunch today."

"Thanks."

While eating, Elena becomes curious about Mike and asks, "Mike, do you mind if I ask about you?"

"No, not at all. My parents moved to the States when I was three. My dad studied law right after we settled down in the States. He is working as a lawyer and my mom is a stay-at-home mom because of her health. I have a younger brother. We've lived in several different cities."

"I see." Lily and Elena respond.

"Well, you know what? I searched for the place and found it. I mean, the nursing home where my grandma might be staying. I'm gonna go to see her."

"Oh, that sounds great. I'd love to go with you if you want. Mike, you too?"

"Sure."

"Oh, thanks a lot," Elena gives them a big smile.

"Alright!, then, I'd better call the office to be sure that Grace is there."

Elena makes a phone call to 'Love and Care' and smiles, nodding to show that she called the right place.

When they get off the bus and see the sign, 'Love and Care', they're surprised that it is just a half-hour drive away.

Elena says excitedly, "Oh, it's close, huh. I can commute every weekend if she needs me."

"But, can she recognize you if she has dementia?" Lily asks.

"Let's see."

They push the big glass door of the the nursing home and look around the small lounge that looks cozy along with an indoor garden. Elena points at a bunch of lilies on the reception desk.

"Hey, you're there, Lily. They smell sweet," Elena says, winking at Lily.

A middle aged woman comes out of the room behind the desk.

"Hello, good afternoon. What can I do for you?"

"I called you a half hour ago. We're here to meet Ms. Grace Lee."

"Oh, yes. She has been here for a decade. You are ...?"

"I'm her granddaughter and these are my friends."

"Oh, I see. I'm the manager. Put your name and number down in the visitor book, please."

The manager calls out a caregiver in a uniform who is carrying an old lady in a wheelchair to the indoor garden, and asks that residents should stay in their beds after finishing lunch.

"Alright! Now you can go see her. Come this way."

The manager presses the elevator button.

"After you."

Elena, Lily and Mike get off the elevator on the third floor. They are speechless when confronting the unusual scene of elderly patients hobbling down the hall with walkers. Lily looks at Elena with her jaw dropped, and Mike does too.

"Elena, I've never seen these patients. Let's go to Grace quickly. I can't stand this situation."

"Yes, okay."

The manager interrupts their conversation.

"This way, please." The manager takes them to the room at the end of the hall.

At the doorway of the room with the door open, Elena takes a deep breath feeling odd because it is the first time for her to meet her maternal grandmother. The manager points to the bed where Grace is resting, and goes back to the elevator.

Elena sees Grace sit up in her bed by the window. When Elena comes to a halt in front of her, Grace looks up at Elena with a probing look.

"Hi." Elena bows to Grace.

"Do I know you?" Grace asks.

"I think so. I'm Elena, your granddaughter."

Grace seems astonished.

"Who? Elena? Are you serious? Then, you're Julie's daughter? Oh, now Henry's."

"Yes, Henry is my dad."

"Oh, Elena! How can you be here alone?"

"Actually, I'm not alone. I'm here with my friends, Lily and Mike."

"Hello, Ms. Lee. Nice to meet you." Lily and Mike bow to Grace.

Grace looks at them, giving a nod.

Elena pulls a nearby chair up to the bed to sit close to Grace. Lily and Mike also sit on other chairs next to her. For a second, Elena thinks Henry resembles his mother in terms of face shape because Grace in her mid-80s is far from graceful, with an angular face. And she doesn't appear to have dementia.

"Grandma. Can you recognize me?"

Grace is staring at Elena with her lips slightly open.

"Yeah, you've grown up well," Grace says, still in disbelief.

"Thanks, Grandma. By the way, how have you been? I'm sorry to see you live here," Elena says.

"Elena, don't say that. I'm happy living here. You know, I'm old." Grace says, looking at the wall.

"Grandma. Who is Julie? You mentioned that name."

Grace doesn't respond right away. Instead, she just closes her eyes as if she thinks about what is going on in front of her eyes.

Elena holds her tongue and looks around the room. She finds that there are two other elderly women, glancing at them. At last Lily whispers to Elena avoiding their gazes, "They're paying attention to us. I don't think they have dementia."

"Maybe," Elena says with her eyes on Grace.

Grace finally opens her eyes, and then suddenly, Grace begins to cough hard.

Elena turns her head to call a caregiver and Lily stands up to go out.

"No, no. I'm okay. I often cough. It's nothing. Keep your seat."

Grace clears her throat to speak.

"Elena, it's been almost fourteen years since I held you in my arms. You're sixteen, right?"

"Yes, Grandma. It's really nice to find you. Um…" Suddenly, Elena seems to be getting choked up at this moment.

"Well, what brings you in here?"

"Well… I don't know." Elena is evasive.

"Did Henry say anything about me?" Grace asks.

"No. Frankly speaking, last night I just overheard Eva saying I'm Henry's niece. And I was shocked. And, this morning I searched for you and here I am, at last! You know, Henry doesn't know I overheard him."

Grace closes her eyes while listening to Elena. It feels like she wants

Elena to go away. Elena is wondering why Grace tries to avoid talking about the past related to Elena and her birth mother and Henry. Once again there is an awkward silence. Elena decides to wait with patience because she knows that her visit to Grace was sudden. With her eyes cast down, Elena looks at Lily who has been sitting still next to her surfing online, and she sees Mike playing online game. As the clock is ticking, almost twenty minutes have passed. The room is in silence and the other two old women seem to fall asleep.

Elena thinks that it's time to leave Grace alone.

"Grandma, I think I'm bothering you by showing up suddenly. So you might be confused more than I was. Now I know where you are. So, I'll come to you as often as I can."

Grace glances at Elena and says, "Yes, I'm exhausted. But, Elena, I think you'd better not come again."

"One more thing! Don't tell Henry that you came and saw me. Never! Okay?"

"What? Why?" Elena asks with surprise.

"Don't ask. And live as Henry's daughter, as you have before. My little sweetie! I love you. Good bye!" Grace says and holds Elena's hands.

Then, Grace slides into bed and closes her eyes.

Elena can't help but leave the room.

"Alright, Grandma. I'm leaving now, but I'll come back to you someday. Don't worry I'll have a permission from you in advance. And

I won't tell anyone about this visit. Bye, take care!."

Grace doesn't answer Elena, and she opens her eyes after she senses that Elena has gone. With her eyes fixed on the ceiling, Grace begins to recall the past fourteen years. Up to now, Grace has been at peace, adapting herself to the nursing home life. But all of a sudden, she feels her mind racing with thoughts that things will never be the same after she saw Elena. All the years she has gone through come to mind and the situation in which she can't do anything as an old lady is bitterness itself.

About fourteen years ago when Elena was two years old, Grace was lonely without her remarried husband but was happy with her two grown-up children, Julie and Henry. Though Julie was the daughter of her husband's former spouse, Grace cared for her more than Henry, her biological son. And Grace had been relying on Julie psychologically after the loss of her husband who died of cancer. While living near Julie who had worked as a lawyer, with a joyful heart Grace volunteered to take care of Elena whom Julie gave birth to. Henry also had been good until he got into trouble at the workplace and so, he started his own business after giving up his career. At that time he had been happily married with Eva.

At this point, Grace sighs and sees the woman who is sitting up now in her bed across the room.

"Oh, you look sad. You can talk to me if you want," the old woman says in a weak voice.

"I'd like to, but it's complicated."

"By the way, a painful memory haunts me. I've regretted ever since. I should have taken action in the first place. I was a fool." Grace rambles.

"Oh, poor Grace. You're not as old as I am. You're a 80-something woman. So you can get out of this place and do whatever you want," the woman says to Grace.

"Come to think of it, you're right. But how? And what for? I'm a useless old woman without money. I'd better stay quiet."

"Well, maybe you're right... Actually you are not that young enough to do what you want. Hmm..."

Grace and the woman are speechless and gaze into space in a daze.

A few minutes later, the woman lies on her back and Grace gets out of the room to go to a small garden built in the back yard on the first floor. She sits on a bench and looks through the flowers in the garden. Walking along the garden is her usual routine to breathe fresh air, but now she comes down to chill out.

However, Grace can't help but think back to a time fourteen years ago. Still, Grace shudders as she recalls the horrible car accident Julie had. After the crash, Grace has lost everything; her son-in-law was killed at the scene and Julie was badly injured and died shorty afterward. Grace was so overwhelmed with grief to the point that she wanted to give up on life. But she had their daughter, Elena, who was two years old being left all alone. Grace had to take responsibility for Elena and then made a plan how to raise her. Though Grace didn't have regular income, she had a nice condominium and some extra money to spend for Elena. As Grace made effort to live a normal life with Elena, she was slowly getting over the grief of losing Julie. But it wasn't long before her later life turned into a misery when she realized Henry had become a different person. He pushed Grace to sell her home and her property by telling that he needed money to expand his business. He also told her that he and Eva would adopt Elena asserting that Grace was too old to raise a toddler. Grace was shocked since his attitude changed suddenly, but she had no choice but to accept his suggestion. Grace was powerless without anyone on her side, so she did what Henry said. And then Grace was placed in a nursing home that cares for the elderly and individuals with dementia. Everything around Grace was shattered in about four months after her stepdaughter, Julie, had a car crash. When she began her later life in the nursing home, she decided to bury her feelings about her son, Henry, wishing Elena a happy life.

Grace feels tears dropping on her cheeks for the first time in a long while. Once again, she feels the betrayal that came from Henry, her own son, who she gave birth to. She absolutely understood him because adjusting to life in a blended family couldn't be easy, so she tried to satisfy him with everything she could afford. But he dumped her after she had no one to rely on. She shakes her head to dispel her sadness because Henry is still her son and Elena seemed to be well cared for. In a minute, she wipes the tears from her eyes promising herself that she won't dwell on the past from this moment.

But at this moment, since Grace saw Elena who took after Julie, she finds herself unable to stop missing Julie, her late stepdaughter. And she again feels regret for her absence from Julie's funeral. Speaking of the funeral, she should have attended it to say farewell to Julie and confirmed that Julie was really dead even though Henry forced her not to come. Henry insisted that she couldn't dare face the injured body of Julie and let her go away for good.

All of a sudden, doubts about Henry arise when Grace comes up with the life insurance that her son-in-law had. In a second, Grace tries to let it go thinking it is no use to look back now. She sees a caretaker coming and stands up to get inside.

After a while, Mike, Lily and Elena get off the bus near Lily's place and head to the nearest bakery to have some sweets and soda for a change since they were shocked by the scene of the nursing home where most elderly people lie in their sick beds.

Lily drinks up the Coke in one go and says, "Elena, it was a surprise to see such old people lying in beds. Have you seen those people?"

"No, it's the first time. But looking at them made me feel sad. You know they had once been young," Elena says.

"Lily, what do you think about Grace's reaction? Did you feel the same as I did?" Elena asks.

"You mean, she seemed like hiding something? Yeah, there was a thing you couldn't think about, I guess."

"Maybe. What would that be?" Elena asks.

"One thing is clear. You're not Henry's daughter but his sister's. Grace didn't tell you, though. And Grace doesn't have dementia," Lily says.

"Lily's right. She seems normal. That's why she hides some things from you, Elena." Mike says.

"Well, I'm really wondering where my real mom is. What if she is a dead person?" Elena says.

"Then, why didn't Grace tell you the truth? Instead of it, she asked you not to come again. What is she afraid of?" Lily says with a curious look.

"Anyway, I don't care what she's afraid of. I'll go and see her again," Elena says.

"Right, but you'd better not tell Henry that we've visited Grace like she said. I guess there is a reason," Lily says.

Elena is tilting her head and says, "Hmm. Henry is a mysterious man."

After drinks, they decide to spend the afternoon doing their own work. But, before then, Mike says, "Hey, do you wanna go to an indoor rock climing gym?" Elena shows an interest in it, but Lily says that she has things to do with Elena at home glancing at Elena who can't ignore her gaze.

"How about next Saturday?" Elena asks.

"Okay. And... Elena, can I have your cell number?" Mike asks.

"Sure, here you go."

After parting ways, Elena accompanies Lily to help with math problems. At the elevator door, they bump into a woman.

"Oh, Mom! What a rush!" Lily says with a surprise.

"Oh, Sweetie!" Nora, Lily's mother, says, looking over at the parking lot.

"Is anyone waiting for you?" Lily asks.

"Yep. My friend. Hi, Elena, we see every day, huh," Nora says, smiling.

"Hi, Ms. Yoo." Elena bows to Nora.

"Lily, I'm going out to get some air. Okay, girls! Have a nice time." Nora dashes out of the sliding glass door.

Lily and Elena briefly glance at Nora's back, and at that point Elena sees a car making a U-turn in which a driver seems like Henry.

"Hey, did you see the driver?"

Elena asks when they step into the elevator.

"No, why?"

"I'm not sure, but he looked like my dad."

"Really?" Lily says.

"You know what? Yesterday, I saw my dad at the gate when you were on the phone. I stopped him and he said he had to meet someone who had business with him," Elena says.

"Hey, it sounds crazy, but what if my mom is dating your dad?"

"What? No! But, wait a minute! You may be right. Then, Henry's having an affair with your mom?" Elena almost shouts.

"Nah, I was joking." Lily laughs.

"But, you never know. I've never imagined Henry is my uncle." Elena lets out a sigh.

"Come to think of it, it could be possible. Elena, let's find out if Henry is cheating on Eva because of Nora!"

"How?"

Elena and Lily look at each other.

"First of all, we should know which high school they went. I know the one my mom went. How about you?" Lily asks.

"Well, I think I know too."

And they find that Henry and Nora went to the same high school. Lily blinks her eyes and says, "Elena, I'll ask my mom about her boyfriend's name and then I'll text you."

"Okay! By the way, we had so many things today, didn't we?" Elena says.

"Yeah, you're right. It was your private family issue though," Lily says.

"I wish I could go back to last year. It's too much to bear." Elena says in a gloomy mood.

"Come on! You have me and Mike too. I think he would like to be your friend."

Elena leaves Lily's condo late at night. Though there is no one in sight, Elena doesn't feel afraid. She checks her cell phone again to see if there is any message from Eva. She takes deep breaths to soothe herself. Now Elena knows that Eva's frosty attitude toward her hasn't started for no reason, which results in the finding of the truth of her birth. As she gets close to her home, Grace's face comes to her mind. She is wondering why she has to keep quiet about the visit to the nursing home. She shakes her head feeling confused. The more she struggles to think about what happened between Grace and Henry, the deeper she sinks to a state of chaos.

Elena looks around when hearing the voice of Henry.

"Hey, Dad. You're home late. It's Saturday."

"Yeah, but I'm coming from work." Henry smiles at Elena.

Elena looks at him thinking that he is, as usual, nice and caring though she knows now that he is her adoptive dad as well as her uncle.

"I can't believe you're my uncle." Elena mumbles.

"Are you talking to me, Elena?"

"No!" Elena smiles.

"Isn't your mom home yet, huh?" Henry says when Elena switches on a light in the living room.

"Dad, you'd be better off calling her." Elena says and goes to her room.

Several days have passed since visiting Grace. Elena still tries to endure Eva who keeps giving the cold shoulder. Eva gets out of the way when Elena is around. Henry is at work from dawn till night, and Eva never talks to Elena treating her as if she doesn't exist at home. Deep down, Elena is really upset, but even so, Elena always says hi to Eva.

On Saturday morning, Elena walks past Eva who is watching TV in the living room.

"Mom, I'm leaving. If you want, I can go shopping with you. Today's Saturday," Elena says kindly with a sweet smile.

As expected, Eva just glances at Elena without any words.

"Okay, bye, Mom,"

Elena shuts the front door behind her. Feeling defeated, she swallows her tears and heads toward the library. These days, Elena doesn't spend her weekends at home because Eva makes her feel suffocated in the house. While walking down the street, she thinks of Lily and Mike who live normal lives compared to Elena herself. Only last week were they together when visiting Grace, but it feels like she saw them a month ago.

Elena stops by a convenience store to have a sandwich for breakfast. She sits on a stool at the window table. She looks at her cell phone to see if she gets any message from Lily about the name of Nora's boyfriend which Lily was supposed to text. Elena assumes that she might make Lily feel uncomfortable regarding her private life. Lily has nothing to do with Grace and Henry even though she is Elena's close friend. Then, Elena sees a call from the nursing home, 'Love and Care.'

"Hello, may I speak to Elena Lee?"

"Speaking. Is that you, the manager?"

"Yes, this is Ms. Kim. You visited here last Saturday."

"Yes, is there any problem with my grandma, Grace?"

"No, she is just fine. But yesterday she asked me to call you to say you can visit her whenever you want."

"Really? She said that?"

"Yes, she wanna see you. I think she missed you a lot after you'd visited her."

"I see. How is she now? I mean her brain and body health," Elena asks.

"As usual. She rarely speaks, but she is doing okay. I hope to see you soon." Ms. Kim hangs up the phone.

Elena sits still wondering what made Grace change her mind. She definitely didn't want Elena to come again.

A minute afterward, a message pops up. It reads "Elena, it's me,

Mike. Shall we go see a movie this afternoon?"

Elena texts him back.

"Mike, Is Lily going with us?"

"No, she is supposed to meet her friend." Mike texts Elena.

"Oh, then, how about going rock climbing?" Elena texts.

"Sounds good. I'll meet you at 3 at the bus stop we got off."

"Yep, see you soon."

After eating up her sandwich, Elena gets on the bus to go see Grace before meeting Mike. While riding in the bus, Elena thinks of Lily, and can't help feeling upset since Lily is busy with her friends from school. At that moment a picture pops up with a text.

"Here is a picture of my mom with her boyfriend. Is he Henry?"

Elena sees Henry on the picture with her eyes wide open.

"Oh my God! It's him, Henry. What the heck is happening right now?"

"Why is it Henry who Nora picked for a boyfriend?" Lily texts.

"Well, but you know there is nothing we can do," Elena texts.

"Anyway, don't tell Eva. It's none of our business," Lily texts.

"Got it. Lily, have a nice weekend. Keep in touch."

Elena opens the door of the nursing home and sees Ms. Kim getting off the elevator.

"Oh, you came right away. Grace will be happy with you," Ms. Kim says.

"I guess so."

"Do you wanna meet her here instead of her room?" Ms. Kim asks.

"But... can she come down here alone?" Elena asks.

"Absolutely. She usually spends her afternoon in the outdoor garden."

Ms. Kim makes a phone call to one of the caregivers on the floor that Grace stays.

"The lunch is at noon for one hour." Ms. Kim says before going back to her office room.

Elena is standing in front of the elevator to help Grace in walking. But she is a bit surprised when she sees Grace walk like a normal person.

"Grandma, you look great," Elena says, smiling.

"Thanks. I missed you a lot. I was sorry to say not to come again."

"Don't say that. I didn't mind it," Elena says.

"Okay, let's go to a cafe nearby. I got a permission."

Grace and Elena sit at the window-side table with a view. Elena stands up in order to get some drinks.

"Grandma, what would you like to drink?" Elena asks.

"Just a glass of milk."

Elena sits on her chair with a glass of milk and a soda.

"Well, how's your school going? You're a high school freshman, right?" Grace says, looking at Elena in the eyes.

"Yes. I am. Grandma, you look normal enough, but you're living in the nursing home. It's odd to me."

"Well... Hmm." Grace sips milk.

"I think there is a story," Elena says.

"Well, yeah, there is. But you're too young to understand," Grace says, feeling some sort of conflict within herself.

"Elena, are you happy with Henry and Eva? If yes, you'd better not know the truth."

"What makes you say that?" Elena asks.

"Because I want you to have a normal and happy life," Grace says.

Elena stares at Grace wondering what kind of truth it will be.

"You know, if I didn't overhear Henry, I wouldn't know that I was his niece and I would never tried to find you. And if Eva didn't turn her back on me, sitting with you right now wouldn't happen," Elena says.

"What? Oh my gosh! I thought she loved you."

"Yes. She did, but changed after knowing Henry is cheating on her."

"Oh my poor baby." Grace pats Elena on the shoulder, stretching her hand across the small table.

Elena almost chokes up with emotion when feeling the warmth from Grace.

"By the way, is Henry having an affair? I can't believe it. I thought Eva was his soul mate."

"Yes, he's seeing my best friend's mom." Elena nods.

Grace sighs and says, "Well, I don't know what to say about that. But one thing is clear. Do study hard, Elena."

"Grandma, can I ask about my birth parents?"

"Well... I love you so much, so I really don't wanna see you get your heart broken."

"But don't worry. I think I'm ready," Elena says.

Grace takes a sip of milk and begins to say about the tragic car crash that Elena's birth parents had. Before going on with the rest of the accident story, Grace studies Elena's face which has turned red with a mix of sorrow and frustration.

"Elena, shall we talk about other things?"

"No. Just keep going. So did they die after the crash?" Elena asks.

"Hmm. Your dad was killed at the scene, and Julie, your mom, was severely injured." Grace stops talking.

"Grandma, has she been hospitalized since then?" Elena asks with her eyes wide open.

"I don't think so. I heard Julie passed away and a funeral proceeded quickly thereafter." Grace turns her face to the window and looks outside.

"Oh, Grandma, you didn't go to the funeral? Why? She was your daughter."

"You know, I was a fool. I should have seen my lovely daughter for the last time, but I had no courage to do that," Grace says with her eyes glued on the table.

"Oh, well, I understand... And then, you let Henry adopt me as his daughter. Now I get it," Elena says with the sad face.

"Elena, listen. I brought you home at first, but Henry took you away from me."

At once Grace thinks that she made a mistake, but it is too late.

"Really? Why?"

"He said I was too old to raise you about two months after the funeral," Grace says, walking on eggshells.

Elena sits speechless without looking at Grace and silence falls over them. About a couple of minutes later, Elena says, "Grandma, it's half past eleven. Let's get going."

"Okay, are you going home?"

"No, I'll be hanging out with my friend," Elena says.

"Good for you, Elena," Grace says.

On the bus ride home, Elena stares outside blankly as if she gets hurt from a blow to the head. What Elena heard about her real parents was a shock in itself, and she can't concede the reality of their death which seems surreal. At the same time, Elena is also sad for them who were so unfortunate as to lose their lives at such a young age leaving their only child, herself. All of a sudden, she feels her eyes well up, missing her parents badly though there is no chance of seeing them, and she doesn't notice that the bus is going past her bus stop. When the bus arrives at the terminal she finds out that she has passed it. She gets off the bus and sees the countryside which is about a twenty-minute drive from her house. Right away, she walks to the next bus which is ready to leave, checking her cell phone messages.

There is one text message from Mike. "Hi, it's me. I have time now. Are you available now?"

Elena texts, "In twenty minutes."

After sitting on the bus seat, Elena looks outside to see where she is. The location of the bus terminal is in a rural area, featuring rustic houses. Out of those houses, she sees a one-story building that looks like a warehouse. As she looks around it, she wonders how she can see the secluded area, just a 20-minute bus ride from her home. Soon, the bus departs on schedule and she takes her eyes off the rural scene to look at her cell phone. At that moment she catches a glimpse of a Volvo passing by the bus toward the one-story building. She mumbles, "It looks like my dad's car." During a ride, she thinks of Henry who has been good to her as her dad now. She texts Henry, "Dad, I have something to ask." There is no response with her message unchecked.

About twenty minutes after leaving the bus terminal, Elena sees Mike waiting for her.

"Oh, Elena, you are bang on time. Let's grab lunch."

"Yeah, I'd like a light lunch," Elena says.

In a few minutes, Mike and Elena sit in a fast food restaurant near a rock climbing gym.

"Elena, how are you doing in school?"

"It's going okay. And you?"

"Nothing new. How is your mom? Is she still cold to you?" Mike asks.

"Yep."

"Well, I went to see my grandma this morning," Elena says plainly.

"Really? She didn't want you to come."

"Yeah, but I got a phone call from the manager. So... but I'm upset now."

"How come? You like your grandma, right?" Mike says with his eyes wide open.

"You know, I was wondering whether my birth parents were alive or not," Elena says, looking away from Mike.

"What happened to them?"

"Well, both of them passed away in a car crash."

"Oh, I'm so sorry for them, Elena."

"Yeah... I was an orphan at the age of two. And I was adopted by Henry, my dad now."

"After knowing that, I feel so sad and helpless. My life sucks," Elena sighs.

"Elena, don't say that. Henry raised you with love, right?"

"Mike, guess what? As I presumed, Henry is dating with Lily's mom, Nora. Lily sent me a photo of Nora with her boyfriend. It was Henry."

"It's ridiculous," Mike shouts out.

"But there's nothing you can do anyway. Well, well, let's go rock climbing now!"

There are quite a few people in the indoor climbing gym which is spacious enough to feature tall climbing walls, bouldering terrain and a course for speed climbing. Most of them crawl up the wall to reach as high as they can, but fall off in the middle. When Mike helps Elena to wear equipment, she can't take her eyes off them.

"Wow! They're doing well," Elena says.

"Elena, listen! Just do what I say."

"Got it."

Mike shows Elena how to climb the wall grabbing a small rock one by one. Elena does as Mike instructs, and so she climbs up by grabbing a rock with her fingers and planting her foot on it. She reaches above the middle of the wall at first try, and then she falls off.

"Great!" Mike says with his thumb up.

"Thanks. It's fun and make me feel better." Elena gives Mike a big smile.

Elena and Mike spend the whole afternoon in the gym trying several climbing courses. Elena seems to forget about the death of her real parents that comes to mind from time to time. When Elena gets exhausted, she gives a gesture to tell Mike that it's time to go home.

"Mike, it was really fun to do rock climbing. Thanks."

"Sure. Let's do this on Saturdays." Mike winks at Elena.

"By the way, I hate to go home."

"Oh, well, I don't know what I can do for you," Mike says with a worried look.

"Don't worry. I won't get away from home."

"And, now I have a place to reduce my stress. So I feel better. By the way, I was wondering why you're nice to me," Elena says, smiling at Mike.

"Well, I was looking for an excise buddy and you know, it was you."

Mike chuckles.

"Oh, one more thing. You looked familiar to me at first sight. I don't know why. Maybe it is because you have a forlorn look occasionally as my mom does," Mike says.

"Really? Hmm. Interesting," Elena says.

The summer break starts with hot sunny days. Elena walks out of the classroom, feeling proud of herself. She has gone through hardships since spring, but she has come out stronger getting good grades in all subjects. When thinking of Eva who made her feel heavy all the time before flying to Canada, Elena feels upset, but, in some way, she feels a sense of relief after Eva's absence. Elena studies hard and does indoor rock climbing to pass the time on weekends. She also goes to the nursing home to see Grace who always would like to hear about the things around her. Grace now knows that Eva left without filing for divorce because Henry made Eva give up a legal divorce by laying all the blame on himself and promising financial support. Even though Elena tells Grace about herself and her surroundings, she doesn't bring up the issue about the past in connection to her real parents.

During the summer vacation, Elena goes to the community library everyday to get ready for the second semester of her first year in high school. One day, Henry and Nora show up at the library's reading room. Elena doesn't imagine him coming to see her though she was asked her whereabouts by him a few minutes ago.

"Oh, Dad." Elena says with a surprise.

At the moment, Lily is back from the restroom and says, "Oh, Mom. What a surprise! How come you're here with Elena's dad."

Both Elena and Lily pretend not to know their relationship.

"Don't look at me like that. We're here to tell that I just joined Henry to be his business partner," Nora says.

"Cool!" Elena and Lily tell a white lie to Nora.

"Thanks. How about having dinner together tonight? Today is Friday," Nora says.

"Urm.., what do you think?" Lily looks at Elena.

"Sounds good."

"Then, see you both at the shopping mall at 6."

After Henry and Nora are out of sight, Lily look at Elena and says, "Are they gonna announce their wedding?"

"Who knows?"

And soon afterwards, they leave the library to wander around the shopping mall.

While snooping around retail stores in the mall, they find Mike browsing in the cell phone shop.

"Hi, Mike. What's up?" Elena asks.

"I was just walking around. My parents went on a trip to Tokyo with my brother and they'll be back tomorrow."

"Then you're gonna eat alone, right? Then join us for dinner," Lily says.

"Cool! Thanks."

"You don't mind having dinner with my dad and Lily's mom, do you?"

"No problem. I'd love to talk with old-school guys." Mike smiles at them.

Elena, Lily and Mike go to a restaurant located on the fourth level of the mall.

Henry and Nora are seated at a round table, studying the menu. They look so intimate like a couple even though they insist that they are business partners.

"Mom. We invited Mike to dinner. We just came across him," Lily says.

"Hi, Mike! We're happy to have dinner together. How are your parents?" Nora says.

"Fine, thanks. And they'll be back home tomorrow from their trip," Mike says to Nora.

"Hello, Mr. Lee. Nice to meet you. Elena and I hang out at the indoor rock climbing gym every weekend." Mike bows to Henry.

"Oh, I didn't know Elena went rock climbing." Henry says looking at Elena.

"Dad, you always came home late." Elena looks at Henry sideways with narrowed eyes.

"That's true. Sorry for that, Elena."

During dinner, Henry looks excited by telling about his businesa introducing some types of goods that he manages and trades in. This time Elena gets to know that Henry is involved in selling and trading household electric appliances and knick-knacks. When he says about the warehouse, Elena thinks of the building that she saw near the bus terminal a month ago.

"Speaking of the warehouse, I bought it with the land this spring. And Nora invested her life savings in my business and she'll get a share from the company profits," Henry says, looking at Nora.

"What? Mom, your life savings? Then, did you save some for my education?" Lily's eyes are widened in shock.

"It must be my daughter to say so, huh. Sweetie, don't worry about your schooling, okay? You'll go to college in the States," Nora says with a warm voice.

"OK. Mom. No offense." Lily shrugs.

"Ha ha, Lily, you're smart," Henry smiles at Lily glancing at Elena.

Elena doesn't seem to care about whatever Henry says.

After Henry finishes, Mike starts to speak about his family. His parents are highly educated and he is the older one of their two sons. His father has worked as a company lawyer making a good salary, and he is also a family man, especially treating his mother like a queen. His father has always taken a good care of her since she had a kidney problem after she had given birth to his younger brother. Now she is in good health, but still his father is worried that she may become vulnerable to a different illness.

After listening to Mike, Henry looks him closely and says, "Is she working?"

"No. I heard my mom had worked as a paralegal, assisting my dad with legal research at a law firm. My dad said he was lucky to have her at the workplace, and then they tied the knot. They love each other a lot. My mom is really a warm-hearted person. She is always ready to help those in need as far as I know." Mike answers to Henry.

"I see," Henry says, tilting his head.

Dinner doesn't last long, so Mike, Lily and Elena left Henry and Nora at the restaurant to enjoy the evening together. After Henry watches them walk away, he looks around and says to Nora, "Let's go grab a tea."

Henry and Nora sit at a cafe, with teas in front of them. Nora takes her cellphone out of her bag, and Henry just stares at the table, spaced out. Through Mike's family story, Henry is reminded of Julie after a long time. When Henry heard Mike talking about his mother, he thought to himself what if Julie flew to America. He doesn't want to look back on the past, but the fact that Julie disappeared without a trace is still a mystery. Julie, his older stepsister, was smart to be a lawyer and also nice helping him with many things. After his stepfather passed away, Julie supported Grace, his mother, with the cost of living. She was also supportive of Henry. At this point in his reflection, he shakes his head lightly feeling guilty. And then he meets Nora's eyes.

Nora glances at Henry sitting across the table and thinks that he is much quieter than usual. To refresh the vibe, Nora says, "What a quick dinner! At 7:30, it's bright in the summer."

"Yeah, it's still early in the evening," Henry says.

"What makes you have a sulky look?"

"Me? I don't know. Just Mike's mother reminds me of my older sister." Henry says.

"Really? You mean, Julie? I know her, I don't remember her face though. We once bumped into her near your place a long time ago. How is she?" Nora says.

"Oh, but we haven't hung for almost two decades, have we?" Henry stares at Nora.

"Yeah, anyway, I remember she became a lawyer when we were high school seniors." Nora says to Henry.

"Yeah, but things change. We'd better not talk about her. Nora, did you do research on decorative items women are interested in?" Henry moves on to another topic.

"Yep, I'll email them to you." Nora says to Henry who doesn't seem to be listening.

"Hey, are you having any trouble?" Nora asks.

"No, I'm feeling a bit tired, but I'm alright," Henry says, sipping tea.

"Well, you'd better get some rest." Nora stands up to put her empty cup back on the counter. Henry follows her after he texts Elena to say not to come home late.

Henry drops off Nora at her home and goes to a nearby bar. Once Julie crosses his mind, he can't help but think about the days when Julie and her husband had a car accident.

About seventeen years ago, Henry started his business after leaving the company, and as a result, needed money. Although Julie provided him with financial support by taking out a loan on her condominium, which was a huge thanks to her, Henry tried to scrap up the money. Then, one day when Elena was two years old, he received a phone call from the police, informing him that Julie was in the hospital and her husband died at the scene of the car accident. He was shocked by the tragedy at first, and comes up with some insurance money in his brother-in-law's death. He hurried to the hospital to see Julie. According to the doctor's diagnosis, she had a minor concussion but no injuries on her limbs. She needed a few days to recover, but she fell into a semi-comma. So Henry and his mother, Grace, held a funeral for Julie's husband without Julie. Grace was devastated at that time, fearing she might lose Julie too. Several days after the funeral, Henry and Eva visited Julie, wishing that Julie would not have regained consciousness. They looked down at her in the sick bed, whispering that they would adopt Elena if Julie would not regain her strength. And they talked in a low voice about how they would take advantage of the insurance coverage benefits. At dawn the following morning, Henry visited Julie alone while Eva went to work. And to his astonishment, Julie vanished from the hospital bed. He hurried over to the nurses' station and asked if Julie had been discharged. The answer was no, and the administration office called the insurance company and the police as well. But now Julie remains classified as a missing person. He still doesn't understand how she went missing.

Reminded of Julie, Grace suddenly flashes in his mind. To this day, Henry hasn't thought of Grace after he placed her in the nursing home. He feels no emotion toward her. By paying for the nursing home fees, he thinks he is doing the best for his mother who cared for her remarried husband's daughter, Julie. Whenever he recalls his childhood, he feels sorry for himself because he barely felt secure in the blended family; consequently, he became indifferent toward Grace. So he didn't care about how Grace could be devastated when he took Elena from her who already had been overwhelmed with grief from Julie's death, which he lied about, covering up the truth. Still, he doesn't feel sorry for Grace, his mother, but has cared about Elena who isn't technically related by blood.

At this time of remembering the past, Henry sighs softly and checks the current time in Canada.

"Hey, babe, how are you doing? Anything new?" Henry calls Eva.

"No, nothing special. But I applied for a math teaching position." Eva says over the phone.

"Really? Oh, right. You have a permanent resident card!" Henry says.

"By the way, are you sure you'll be closing your business soon?" Eva asks.

"Yes, I wanna live with you and Evan. Are you still mad at me? I hope not."

"You know, I almost forgot what you did. It could happen to me. And we are soul mates, right?" Eva says in a chuckling voice.

"Then, can I ask you to apply for citizenship for me?"

"I already did it in case. The citizenship process is underway." Eva giggles.

"What? Oh, Eva, you're cute!" Henry says with joy.

"Eva, well... I'm burdened by Elena. She's too young to be left alone here. What do you think of it?" Henry asks.

"It's none of my business. She's your niece. Grace can live with her," Eva says.

"Alright! I'll take care of it."

"Honey, I'm trying to collect money." Henry says in a whisper.

"You mean, by closing your business?" Eva asks.

"Sort of" Henry replies calmly.

After a few more chats, Henry hangs up the phone.

12

As autumn begins and the leaves turn, Elena finds herself alone again. The days when she enjoyed hanging out with Lily and Mike as a threesome were like a dream to Elena. Elena feels scared being home alone though she comes home late to sleep only. Since Henry drops by to check on Elena whether she is doing okay without sleeping at home, it seems like Elena lives alone in a large place. As days go by, she gets more lonesome even missing Eva who left without a hug.

At last, Elena comes up with an idea that Grace is the only one that can replace Eva. To bring Grace home, Elena must contrive a way to get consent from Henry who may never imagine that Elena is seeing Grace. Elena knows that it doesn't seem easy since the situation is complicated, but she decides to take an action one way or another.

One Saturday in late September Elena goes to Grace and takes her to the cafe.

"Grandma, I have something to tell you."

"Sweetie, what is it?"

"You know, I haven't told you this because I thought you must be worried about me. Grandma, I can't be home alone every day and night. Dad comes home once in two weeks, but no sleeping at home. Of course, I have no problem with money, but I can't live like this. So, I want you to come home and live together," Elena says.

"But Henry doesn't know you're coming to see me. And he hasn't been good to me except paying for my nursing home fees," Grace says.

"He took my money." Grace blurts.

"What? What are you talking about? He took your money and put you here against your will?" Elena asks with her eyes wide open.

Grace nods, looking outside the cafe window.

"Oh! I can't believe it. You haven't said anything bad about him. He has been nice to me. How could he do a real bad thing to you? Wait a minute, then, I was adopted by him because of money. Hmm…" Elena almost groans.

Suddenly, Elena slaps her knees and says, "What if he adopted me to take money from the insurance company?"

"Well, I think your parents had life insurance on themselves in case they died young. But don't even think like that. Elena, Henry raised you well and still loves you as a dad, right?" Grace gives Elena a smile.

"Yes, Grandma. By the way how can I tell Dad about you?"

Grace just looks at Elena gently and says, "Sweetie, listen to me. We'd better stay as we are. You know things will be very complicated.

Just keep texting me whenever you get home as if I'm with you. How about that? And absolutely you're not alone."

Elena stares at Grace and nods in agreement.

"Yeah, right. I wanna chat every night. But I come home after 10 o'clock and I think you should sleep early," Elena says, frowning at Grace.

"Don't worry. I'll wait for your call every night, Sweetie." Grace grabs Elena's hands.

Elena looks at Grace for a few seconds and says, "Okay, Grandma. I'll do as you say."

On the way home Elena thinks of Henry who has been a nice and honest dad so far. But she can't understand why he was so harsh to his own mother, Grace. Elena is afraid that Henry could do harm to her someday. But soon, Elena recalls a fixed smile that Henry always has given to her, and decides to forget about what he did to Grace.

After visiting Grace, Elena soon gets used to be home alone at night. Whenever she feels upset, she texts Grace, who has always been on hold.

Elena's new way of living in the second semester of her first year of high school results in her getting excellent grades in her final exam. Being proud of herself, Elena tells Grace about her achievement first, and she texts to Lily and Mike who give praise right away. Then, Elena is asked by Mike if she would accept his parents' invitation to a

Christmas lunch. She asks, "Did they invite me alone?"

"No, with your dad, and Lily with her mom too," Mike says.

"Oh, I see. I'd love to. Say thanks to your mom," Elena says.

Christmas is near at hand. Elena tries to tell the invitation to Henry, but she can't reach him. There was no congrats messages about her good grades even after Elena texted to Henry several times. Elena feels a little upset worrying about Henry, and the Christmas season last year crosses her mind. Elena had wonderful time with Eva, Henry and Evan who came over from Canada. Now Elena can't help but feel somewhat deserted while waiting for a call from Henry wondering what is happening to him.

On Christmas Day, Elena still hasn't got any message from Henry, and she calls Mike early in the morning.

"Hi, Mike. I don't think I can make it to the party cuz my dad is out of reach."

"Really? It's odd. Then, you can come alone. We don't care. My parents want to see you anyway," Mike says.

"Alright. Can you tell me your address?"

"Yep. And I'll be waiting at the bus stop at noon."

"Got it." Elena hangs up the phone.

Elena gets off the bus and looks around the neighborhood where only single-family houses are stood. While waiting for Mike at the bus stop, Elena feels an atmosphere of peacefulness and quietness. A few minutes later Elena walks up to Mike who is approaching her, and then they walk down a couple of blocks. Mike stops at the entrance door of the Hong's house.

"Here we are," Mike says.

"Oh, you're living in a big house." Elena looks at the house over the low fence.

"Yep. After you." Mike says, opening the entrance door.

While walking across the front yard, Elena turns her face to Mike and says, "It may sounds ridiculous, but I feel like I've been here some time ago. It's odd. Actually, I've never been to this neighborhood."

"Yeah? My dad rented this house and we moved last year. Maybe it's because you live only ten-minute drive from this place," Mike says, smiling.

"Maybe…"

Since it is December, there is no vitality in the yard of the house because of the bare branches of a tree and the lawn which has turned brown. But the yard is bright, with a southern exposure that provides plenty of sunshine.

Mike holds the front door open to let Elena get in the house. When Elena takes off her snickers, she hears Lily calling her name outside of the door. Mike opens the door again for Lily.

"Mom, Dad, my guests are here," Mike says loudly.

In a second, Mike's parents come out of the kitchen and give Elena and Lily a big smile.

"Hi, Lily."

"Oh, you are Elena. It's very nice to meet you. And I'm happy to have you here," Sunny, Mike's mother, says.

"Hello, Mr. and Mrs. Hong. Nice to meet you. And thank you for inviting me," Elena says.

"Hi, Merry Christmas!" Alex, Mike's father, says to both girls with a smile.

After greeting each other, Lily says to Sunny that Nora will show up a little later. Sunny nods and says, "You guys, just hang around until lunch is ready, and we have a few more guests."

"Mrs. Hong, could I give you a hand?" Elena asks.

"Oh, how thoughtful of you! But no thanks. Just make yourself home."

Sunny and Alex go back to the kitchen and Mike takes Elena and Lily to his bedroom. Lily sits on the window seat, opposite the bed and says, "Elena, where is your daddy? My mom said she couldn't contact him for several weeks."

"Oh, Lily, what are you talking about? Then, Henry disappeared?" Mike asks.

"Sort of. So far, he hasn't taken my call. What if there was something wrong with him?" Elena says with a worried look.

"Is his business going well?"

"I have no idea."

"Lily, do you know what's going on with him? I think your mom knows about it," Mike says.

Lily shrugs her shoulders saying, "I don't think so."

"Okay, let's talk about something else. Elena, you live on your own in a large place, right?" Mike says.

"Yep, since summer. So I'm used to it." Elena shrugs without any emotion.

"Yeah, but it isn't easy. You're really mature. Well, it's winter vacation, so how about making a plan to go skiing."

"Okay, I'm always available," Elena says.

"Lily, you'll go skiing too, okay?" Mike confirms with Lily.

"Yep! Now, I'm hungry. Let's go downstairs!" Lily says.

When they get downstairs, they see Nora helping Sunny by setting the lunch table. Nora glances at them and says to Lily, "Come place cutlery on the table. Lunch is almost ready. There are ten people."

The big table is set for lunch. When sitting between Mike and Sunny, Elena feels cozy and comfortable as if she is a family member of the Hongs. After saying grace, everyone at the table starts to eat.

"Oh, everything tastes amazing." All the guests say to Sunny.

"Thank you. I'm happy to hear that," Sunny says.

"Mrs. Hong, it feels like food is from the heart," Elena says to Sunny.

"Really? Thanks. Help yourself."

"Yes, I haven't eaten these kinds of food for a long time," Elena says.

"Oh, right! I heard about your mom from Mike." Sunny looks at Elena.

Elena feels like she is wrapped by the warm blanket, and she's almost likely to shed tears. But she says calmly with a smile, "My mom is in Canada. She may be quite busy there."

"And I'm doing okay without her. I always eat out alone though."

"Oh… feel free to come to my house," Sunny says.

Elena smiles at Sunny, nodding.

After the pleasant lunch, Sunny asks the guests to move to the living room for dessert. Nora who has been close to Sunny as school parents stays in the kitchen to clean up the dinner table. Elena just stands near the kitchen sink to do some dishes with Mike who begins to load the dishwasher, but Sunny leads Elena into the living room. Elena sits on the couch next to Lily with other guests who don't pay attention to the young ones.

Elena checks her cell phone waiting for a call from Henry and hears someone speaking to her.

"Hi, I'm Ron Hong, Mike's younger brother. I slept over at my friend's house. So I didn't have a chance to say hello."

"Hi, yeah. What grade are you in?" Elena asks.

"I'm in 7th grade. Mike and I go to the same school. You know, I'll join you to do indoor rock climbing."

"Really? It's good to hear that. Ron, I can teach you how to do it. I'm still working on it though," Elena says with a grin.

"She climbs well." Lily adds.

"By the way, Elena, Ron has your eyes, huh?"

"Hmm. I'm honored to hear that. Ron is a handsome guy." Elena giggles.

And Elena looks at her cell phone again to check the message when Sunny hands out a dish of dessert to her.

"Oh, thanks, Mrs. Hong." Elena grabs it without noticing that there is a call right after the message.

"Elena, your phone is buzzing. It is perhaps your dad," Sunny says.

"Well, I'll call him back later," Elena says.

"Elena, you'd better take it to know where he is now," Lily says.

"Uh? The call is from an unknown number."

"Well, then don't take it."

But Elena rises to her feet and goes to the kitchen to take the call.

"Hello, who's calling?" Elena answers the call.

"...."

"Hello? Hello?" Elena touches the red phone icon to end a call.

"Hmm. There was silence on the call." Elena shrugs her shoulders.

"What if it's your dad, Henry?" Lily says.

"Nah."

"Anyway, Henry has disappeared! Oh boy."

At that moment, Sunny cuts into the conversation.

"Elena, is your dad okay?"

"Maybe. The call was from an unknown number and there was nothing to hear on the other end," Elena says.

"I see. I bet you are worried about your dad. But relax! Everything will be fine." Sunny says, looking Elena in the eyes.

"Thanks."

"Elena, by the way, now I can tell you look familiar. Have I met you before?"

"No, I don't think so," Elena says.

"Were you born in this neighborhood?"

"No, my family moved here when I was a fourth grader. Why are you asking?"

"I'm just curious. That's it."

Elena takes a bite of cake on her dessert plate and says, "What a taste!"

Sunny smiles at Elena.

"I'll pack some for you to take home."

"Oh, thanks a lot, Mrs. Hong."

"No problem. Anyway, you are always welcome at my house." Sunny says, giving Elena a wink and goes to the other side of the living room to join her other friends.

"So, what are we gonna do now?" Lily asks.

"Where is Ron?" Elena asks looking around.

"He's out to hang out with his friends."

"Hey, are we gonna be here for the whole afternoon?" Lily asks again.

"No, let's go see a movie. I booked tickets for three of us." Mike shows them e-tickets.

"Alright! Then..."

Lily stands up to take her stuff before leaving, and sees Elena's cell phone buzzing on the coffee table.

"Elena, you have a call on your cell."

"Don't bother. I won't take it," Elena says.

"But, maybe it can be from your dad," Lily says.

"Okay, okay. Hello? Who's calling?"

"Hello. This is Susan. May I speak to Henry?"

"You've got the wrong number." Elena says quickly and taps the end call button.

"Hey, are you okay? You look a bit weird."

"Well... the call was from a woman."

"Then, there's no problem at all." Lily says and turns around.

"But she called Henry from my number. What's up with Henry?" Elena says to Lily from behind.

"Really? Huh. How long has he been gone?" Mike asks, standing next to Lily.

"About three weeks? I texted him, but no response. I hope he's doing well. Anyway, let's go," Elena says.

Elena can't be easy though she is watching the movie with Lily and Mike. After the movie, three of them stop by the snack bar to have light meals. As soon as sitting at the table, Lily and Mike talk about the film, but it doesn't seem like Elena is in a talking mood.

"Elena, what's the matter with you?" Mike asks.

"You're thinking about the woman, aren't you?"

"Well, the woman's call left me feeling nervous. Why Henry gave her my number as if it were his own? Isn't it odd?" Elena says, glancing at both Lily and Mike.

"Yeah, but I'm sure that he's not dating her. My mom asked me about you and Henry several times and said what if he ran off with her money," Lily says.

At that point, Elena stares at Lily with wide open eyes.

"What? Then she might be a lender. She called Henry to have her money back." Elena wears a worried look on her face.

"Oh, Elena, don't worry. It won't happen," Mike says.

"But if something happens, call me and Lily. What are friends for?" Mike gives a big smile.

The new year has arrived, and Elena still doesn't hear from Henry. At last she decides to tell Grace about Henry. On New Year's Day, Elena sets off to visit Grace, feeling bitter about her current circumstances.

"These days are worse than last spring. If I have no home, where would I go?" Elena mumbles.

All the way down the road to the nursing home, Elena's mind is filled with worries about her future. Elena opens the door and faces the manager who seems to be waiting for her.

"Hi, Elena, how are you doing? I think I have something to tell you about Grace beforehand."

"Oh, you scare me. What is it?"

"Well... the fee didn't come in, so I needed to follow up. By the way I couldn't reach your dad, Henry. So, I was wondering if you could explain about that."

"Oh, really? What a surprise! How behind is he on the payment?" Elena asks.

"Just one month. You know, she needs to pay the fee upfront." The manager says, studying Elena's face.

"I know you're under age. So, I'm asking about your dad. I didn't tell Grace this yet."

Elena looks shocked but says, "I think I should talk to Grace about this. Is she doing okay?"

"Yes, shall I page Grace for you now?" the manager asks.

Elena doesn't answer the manager immediately, feeling sad. A few seconds have passed and Elena says that today is not the right time to see Grace. The manager agrees with Elena and says, "See you around."

Elena walks slowly to the cafe where she has come by with Grace. It seems like Elena needs a space to find comfort for herself. She sits at the window table with a glass of juice. She looks blankly out the window. The view outside the window is the same as the one she and Grace saw before. But now bare trees with leafless branches create a deprived atmosphere, which makes her feel worse than ever.

Elena sits still without drinking Juice for a while and mumbles, "I need to get advice from Mike and Lily."

She texts Lily, "Can we meet up this afternoon?" She gets a response right away: "Alright, at 3 at the mall."

Elena drinks up her juice and springs to her feet to take the bus. As soon as she gets on the bus, she begins to search for the information about a loan secured on the condominium. As a teenager, she has never known about that stuff. But after hearing that Henry didn't pay the nursing home fee for Grace, she recalls the woman who called Henry from her number on Christmas day. Since then she has been feeling dubious about whether the woman gave Henry a loan, with his condo as security. After doing research online, she learns how to look up property rights, and discovers the website for the condominium registry. In less than twenty minutes, she finds out that Henry's condo has been up for auction and the process is complete, which means it has been sold at auction. She can't believe her eyes because she'll have no place to live soon. With frustration, she gazes out the bus window without noticing that she missed her stop. And then, she again reaches the bus terminal and gets off the bus. Instinctively, she looks at the warehouse thinking about the possibility of finding Henry there. But the warehouse doesn't look the same as it did last June. It seems deserted, with overgrown grasses and dirt smudged across its exterior. She guesses that the warehouse may be auctioned off.

Elena arrives at the mall around noon. There are a few people on each floor in the mall since it is a bit early for lunch on New Year's Day. Elena goes to the food court and sits in the corner of the hall. She has no appetite, but needs to eat because of deep emotional suffering. At this moment, she is so upset that nothing can ease her sadness. After ordering food, she touches the gallery on the cell phone. She gazes at each one in the picture of her family who looks happy. Staring at Henry's face, she starts to get angry and feel nauseous. Then, she hears that her food is ready and rises to her feet to get her meal.

When Elena picks up the tray with a hamburger and a Coke on it, she turns around because someone is calling her behind. Surprisingly, she sees Sunny standing with shopping bags.

"Oh, Mrs. Hong. You came here for shopping. Happy New Year!" Elena says.

"Yes, same to you! By the way, you're alone, huh."

"Yes, I went see my grandma this morning," Elena says.

"Does your grandma live near here?" Sunny asks.

"Thirty-minute drive from here," Elena says.

"Oh, I see. I think I heard a little about her from Mike."

Hearing Sunny, Elena walks to her table with the tray in hand. Sunny follows Elena and sits across the table.

"Do you mind if I sit here?"

"Please do." Elena says though she isn't in the mood to talk with others.

"How is your grandma doing? Is she okay?" Sunny asks.

"Yes, she's fine." Elena says, looking around.

"Oh, there, Mr. Hong is coming."

"Yeah. I think I have to go. Elena, see you around!" Sunny leaves for Alex.

As Elena sees Sunny and Alex walk away from her, she feels her eyes filling with tears. But shaking her head, she wipes her tears with her hand and takes a big bite of the burger.

"Stay strong! You can't lose yourself in this chaos!" Elena says to herself.

While eating, Elena is watching online video lecture on language arts. She seems to be trying to return to her usual routine, her face completely engaged in the lesson.

Elena takes her eyes off her cell phone when Lily and Mike sit across the table from her.

"Oh, you both are early."

"Yep. You know, my mom will be with us," Lily says plainly.

"Yeah, I think she knows something about what Henry did," Elena says.

"Do you know what happened to him?" Lily asks with her eyes wide open.

"I still don't know exactly where he is, but he fled somewhere, leaving me alone," Elena answers in a small voice.

In a few minutes, Nora appears with a cup of coffee in hand. Her face looks rigid when her eyes meet Elena's. Noticing a tension between Nora and Elena, Lily attempts to lighten the mood.

"Mom, relax!" Lily says.

"Okay, Sweetie."

"Happy New Year! Ms. Yoo." Elena bows to her.

"Thank you. You too!" Nora smiles a bit at Elena.

"Elena, to speak directly, I have no idea how Henry fled like this. He cashed out by selling his company. I still hold a position, though. I mean, I was transferred to the new owner of the company. Did you happen to know about it?"

"Ms. Yoo, I don't know about his company, but I happened to know about something bad was happening. This morning I went see my grandma, and I heard he delayed the nursing home fee. He is a month behind on the fee payment." Elena says with a grave look and continues, "And I found out by online search that our condominium is sold at action. I think I'll be kicked out soon."

"Oh my God! He left you alone without a place to live! How could a dad did this to his daughter?" Nora furrows her brow.

"Wait a minute, you're his niece. I heard it from Lily last night. If you're Julie's daughter, Henry and you aren't blood relatives, as far as I know," Nora says, blushing.

"What are you talking about? He is related by blood," Elena refutes

Nora's statement.

"Elena, Henry became Julie's brother after his mother remarried. He told me when we went to high school together," Nora says, studying Elena's face.

"It can't be true! You mean, Grace, my grandma isn't my biological grandma? No way!" Elena almost screams.

"Mom! Stop it!" Lily yells at Nora.

"Okay, okay! Elena, I didn't mean to hurt you. I'm truly sorry. But I told you the truth." Nora holds Elena's hands.

Elena says nothing, staring at the table. Mike watches Elena, feeling sorry for her, and Lily looks anxious trying to put Elena at ease. An uncomfortable silence hangs in the air among them.

A little while later, Elena speaks.

"Henry was nice as a dad, but in the end, he fled, though," Elena says in a small voice.

"Anyway, Elena, you can live with us when you have no place to live." Lily speaks, glancing at Nora.

Nora doesn't respond at once but says to Elena, "Well... you're welcome in my home anytime. Feel free to stay with us."

"Are you sure? Thank you so much, Ms. Yoo. If I stay in your home, I'll pay for my living expenses no matter what," Elena says with a look of relief.

At this scene, Mike and Lily remain speechless as if they've lost their tongues. They see Elena as a different person because she looks like she is begging for mercy.

"Elena, you don't have to do that." Nora says, feeling the same way as Lily and Mike do.

Nora continues, "Elena, you know what? I think Henry flew to Eva to live together. So he consolidated all his property and has gone," Nora says.

"What do you mean by that?" Elena asks.

"He gathered all his property together. He already cashed out the condo by getting a loan and sold his company," Nora explains.

Elena nods and says nothing.

Nora wants to talk about the money she invested in expanding his business, but instead, she says, "Elena, don't worry too much. I won't let you be alone anyway."

"Elena, you're Lily's best friend, so adding one more girl to my family will bring joy to our home."

"Well, I have to go now. Guys, Bye for now." Nora rises to her feet and leaves.

After saying bye to Nora, Mike says, "Your mom is so cool! She has accepted Elena as your family."

"My mom is always optimistic. She's a nice person. By the way, Elena, did you tell Grace that her nursing home payment is behind by a month?"

"No, after I heard about it, I was so surprised, so I just left there without meeting Grace," Elena says.

"Yeah, right. How pathetic is Henry?" Mike groans with anger.

"Right! How could leave Elena alone? Did he believe that my mom would take care of her? Then Grace? He is a terrible person!" Lily says in an enraged voice.

Elena doesn't respond to Lily, simply staring at the table. And then, Lily stops talking and Elena opens her mouth and says, "I'm sorry for this unpleasant situation. I know, you both have nothing to do with Henry. But I brought my personal problems to you. I'm so sorry." Elena is close to tears.

"Don't say that! If I were in your shoes, I would do the same as you." Mike comforts Elena, patting her shoulder.

"Alright, guys, what should we do?" Lily boosts the mood.

"Let's go rock climbing!" Mike and Elena reply in unison.

Elena, Lily and Mike arrive at the climbing gym. They are surprised by how many people are inside the gym. Most people gather around top rope climbing area for beginners. They head to the locker room where Mike and Elena have rented a locker from the gym. When Elena gets ready for climbing by wearing rock climbing shoes, she gets a phone call from the manager at the nursing home. The manager says, "Elena, Grace wants to see you today."

Elena replies, "Alright. Now?"

"You can come by any time before 8 o'clock."

"Okay."

Lily looks at Elena while sitting next to each other on the bench.

"This was the manager at the nursing home," Elena explains.

About two hours later, three of them agree to go back home. When they walk to the bus stop, Mike turns to Elena and asks, "Can you stay home alone tonight?"

Elena smiles at Mike instead of replying and keeps walking. In a second Lily holds Elena by the arm and says, "Hey, you can sleep over at my place to adjust to my home."

"Thanks, Lily, but I need to see Grace now," Elena says.

"How come? Ah, today is New Year's Day, so she wants to see your face."

"Yeah, Grace is my grandma no matter what the issue with the blood relations is. Anyway, she raised my late mom. She did a great job." Elena says in a calm voice.

"Oh, you speak like a grown-up, huh." Mike says, smiling.

"Then, we'll come along, Elena."

"No, you both don't have to. I'd better go by myself. Thank you both a lot."

Elena stops by a bakery to eat a sandwich before visiting Grace because it seems to be dinner time at the nursing home. While sitting at the bakery, Elena tries to figure out what she heard from Nora. It is simple to piece together things about her family matter. Grace is Henry's real mother, as well as Julie's stepmother. Therefore, Elena, as Julie's daughter, is related by blood to neither Grace nor Henry. As Elena has this thought, she feels like her life has been a lie.

Elena looks outside through the window of the bakery. It is dark at 6 pm, and all of a sudden, she doesn't want to see Grace when Henry's face comes to mind, thinking--that mother and that son. She lets out a sigh and makes a call to the manager at the nursing home to call off the visit.

After a while, Elena gets off the bus in her neighborhood, walking slowly as she dreads returning home. At last, she texts Lily, "I didn't see Grace. I'm near my place. You know what, I don't wanna go home. What can I do?"

Immediately, Elena gets a text back from Lily, "Come over! I'll be waiting for you."

Lily holds the front door open before Elena rings the doorbell.

"Hi, Elena, welcome home." Surprisingly, Nora exclaims standing behind Lily.

Elena seems to be touched, and so says, "Oh, Ms. Yoo, thank you so much. You're an angel!"

"Yeah? I have an idea. You're staying with us as a tutor for Lily teaching math. How about that?"

"Oh, Ms. Yoo! How thoughtful you are! Thank you. Thank you!" Elena exclaims.

Right away, Elena is led to the vacant room next to Lily's. The room is clean and cozy though it is quite small compared to her room in her family's condo. For now, Elena is content that she has a place to live as long as she wants to stay. Then, she tilts her head wondering if Henry knew Nora would welcome her. At that moment, Lily asks, "What is it? I saw you thinking about something"

"Nah, nothing"

"Let's have dinner. Mom has prepared rice-cake soup," Lily says.

Elena isn't hungry at all, but joins Lily and Nora with gratitude. And then, Elena is spending New Year's evening at Lily's condo with a happy heart.

Meanwhile, Grace stares at her cell phone having half a mind to call Elena after she was told by the manager that Elena canceled her visit and the nursing home fee payment was delayed for a month. At first, Grace was surprised to learn that Henry didn't pay the fee, and next, she felt hurt that Elena didn't want to see her after knowing the fee issue. A minute later, she gets out of her room and goes down to the indoor garden since she has plenty of time left before bedtime.

Grace sits on the bench, looking at a plant blankly. There are several residents who want to enjoy the evening before bedtime. A resident speaks to Grace since she looks so frustrated.

"Excuse me, are you okay?"

"Yes, I'm fine. I was gonna call my granddaughter." Grace shows her cell phone to her.

Instead of calling, Grace texts, "Elena, sweetie, I'm wondering if you're okay. I think there is something wrong with Henry. And don't worry about the fee. I can afford to pay it by myself. Text me back."

And she has waited for a text from Elena until bedtime, but there is no answer.

Two weeks have passed since Elena began to live with Lily and Nora. In the meantime, Elena doesn't call or text Grace because she feels like Grace is no longer her grandmother. The truth that Henry and his biological mother, Grace, are not related by blood makes Elena distant from Grace, especially, when thinking that Henry left her alone without a home. On one hand, she appreciates Henry for raising her with love as her adoptive father, but on the other hand, she can't forgive him for disappearing without a word though he left some money in her bank account to cover her expenses for several months. As she thinks more about him to understand, she feels more disappointed. Besides, she can't be close to Grace because it feels like she became a fool, misled by a lonely old woman. The more Elena looks back on the past year, the more betrayed she feels. Elena had been sad when Eva gave her the cold shoulder and went away to Canada, but then, she became happy with Grace who gave her the courage to study hard while facing the challenges of living alone in a big condo. But now, everything around her seems like an illusion.

During January, Elena goes to the library every day, sometimes with Lily. One day at the end of January, Elena gets a phone call from the manager of the nursing home while she is at the library. The manager asks Elena to come visit Grace, saying that Grace has refused food for several days and there is no need to worry about the fee. Elena doesn't give the manager a yes answer, but says that she might show up sooner or later. After ending the call, Elena is in thought about Grace without any sympathy.

Elena sighs softly looking at Lily who sits across the table in the reading room of the library.

"What is it?" Lily asks.

"The manager told me that Grace has refused food for several days," Elena says in a small voice.

"Oh, really? I'm sorry for her. I think you should go see Grace. I'm happy to go with you," Lily says.

"Thanks, but not now. I'm not up for seeing her. Of course, I'm sorry to hear that Grace has lost her appetite," Elena says.

"Anyway, I need to finish reading this book." Elena says and turns her gaze to the book.

Looking at Elena, Lily rises to her feet to call her mom, Nora.

As soon as Lily steps out, she calls Nora and talks to her about how Grace is in trouble on the phone. Since Grace is Henry's mother, Nora can't ignore her troubles, and so she carefully listens to Lily.

"Mom, I think you'd better ask Elena to visit Grace cuz Elena doesn't wanna see her. I think Elena doesn't care about her after she heard from you about Grace. Elena feels betrayed after learning that Grace has kept the truth about her second marriage a secret from Elena," Lily says over the phone.

"Okay, by the way, I just started having coffee with Sunny. So, it will take at least half an hour to pick you both up," Nora says.

"No problem."

About a half hour later, Lily gets the message from Nora and takes Elena to the parking lot of the library, saying that Nora is waiting for them. Since Elena is grateful to Nora, she follows Lily without hesitation.

Lily opens the rear door of Nora's car and sees Sunny sitting in the front passenger seat.

"Oh, Mrs. Hong. How are you? Are you coming with us?" Lily says, sitting in the rear seat next to Elena.

"Yes. Hi, Elena. How are you doing?" Sunny greets Elena with a glance.

"I'm fine, thank you."

As Nora starts driving, she says to Elena that they are heading to the nursing home.

"Elena, I heard Grace has refused food these days, so I decide to meet her too. And Sunny wanted to come with us when she knew it,"

Nora says.

Elena looks at Nora through the rear mirror and says, "Got it. No problem."

"I already told the manager at the nursing home that we would visit Grace today."

19

Nora pulls her car into the parking lot behind Love and Care sign, and four of them go into the nursing home building. The manager who has attended to a resident greets them with a smile.

"Hi, Elena, long time no see," the manager says.

Elena doesn't smile at her and says, "I know. How is Grace?"

"She just drinks water. You can see her now," the manager says and accompanies the resident to the indoor garden.

Elena takes Nora and Sunny, leaving Lily in the lounge who doesn't want to go see the residents with disabilities living upstairs.

A few minutes later, Elena stops at Grace's bed that is empty wondering where Grace is.

"Oh, she may be in the bathroom. Let's wait. She'll be back soon." Elena says, turning to Nora and Sunny.

At that moment, Elena sees Grace walking toward her.

"Oh, Sweetie, you came see me at last! I missed you so much. Were you too busy to see me?" Grace grabs Elena's hands, ignoring Nora and Sunny.

"I'm sorry, Grandma. You look pale. Please sit on the bed." Elena holds Grace's arm to let her climb into her bed.

After sitting on her bed, Grace looks at two women standing at her bedside.

"Elena, who are they?" Grace asks.

"This is Nora Yoo, Lily's mom, and This is Sunny Hong, Mike's mom."

"Hello." Both women bows to Grace.

Grace gazes at them in confusion.

Immediately, Nora says, "I and Henry went to high school together. You haven't seen me, though."

"I see. By the way, you look familiar..." Grace says, pointing to Sunny.

"Mrs. Lee, I don't think we've met before. But it's nice to meet you," Sunny says.

Grace doesn't respond, just staring at Sunny as if she tries to recall something. A few minutes later, Grace widens her eyes in surprise.

"Wait a minute! You're Julie! You must be Julie!" Grace cries out.

Elena says in surprise, "Grandma! Come on! Are you out of your mind? She is Mike's mother."

Grace looks at Elena dumbfounded.

"Right. Well, sorry for the fuss, Mrs. Hong," Grace apologizes.

"It's okay. You can mistake me for another woman. Mrs. Lee, you should eat well. Please take care of your diet," Sunny says, holding Grace's hand.

"I will. Thank you, Mrs. Hong. Thoughtful!" Grace says and smiles at Sunny, though her eyes remain doubtful.

And then, Grace continues, "Let me tell you this, Elena, don't worry about the nursing home fee payment. I applied for the basic pension a long time ago and I have been receiving it in my savings account."

She swallows and asks, "Is he looking after you, Elena?"

"Well, Grandma, dad has gone somewhere leaving me alone without a home. You know what? Our condo was sold at auction. But luckily, Ms. Yoo allowed me to stay at her place." Elena says, smiling at Nora.

Grace looks startled.

"That's why you didn't come see me. Oh, you should've told me." Grace sighs and shakes her head.

"Nora, how nice of you! From now on, I'll pay for Elena's living costs." Grace says firmly.

Nora doesn't respond to Grace at once, and so, Sunny taps Nora's thigh with her finger.

"Oh, it's good to hear that, but I can afford food cuz there are only three of us at home. Anyway, I'd appreciate it," Nora answers.

Nora wants to tell Grace that how much she has invested in Henry to help expand his company and he fled without giving money back to her. But she knows there is no use in saying that to the old woman in the nursing home.

Nora sighs and says, "Mrs. Lee, don't worry about Elena. I'll take care of her throughout her high school years."

Grace nods in agreement with Nora without saying a word.

At that point, the dinner is served to Grace by a caregiver.

"Oh, it's dinner time. Grandma, do you want me to be with you during the dinner?" Elena asks.

After hearing Elena, Nora says, "We'd better give you both some space. Elena, text Lily when you're ready to leave."

"Mrs. Lee, we're leaving. It was nice meeting you. Take care!"

Then, Nora and Sunny leave the room.

Elena helps Grace grab a spoon and watch her eat. When Grace finishes her meal, Elena says, "Grandma, you have to eat well to stay healthy."

Elena seems to like Grace as her grandmother like before.

Grace looks content, but in a minute, she shakes her head and says to herself, "She is Julie!"

"Elena, if I say this, don't be mad. Sunny really looks like Julie. You know, I've thought of her almost every day since she was gone. So I still remember her face and her way of talking. It was so warm and inviting. Sunny seems just like Julie."

"Grandma! Don't say that, please. She has lived in the States for a long time with her family. She has a husband and two sons," Elena says.

Immediately, Grace nods at Elena, showing her agreement.

"Okay, I won't say that again. I might be wrong."

"Elena, you'd better go now. I was so happy today." Grace hugs Elena tenderly.

Elena joins Lily and other two women who have been waiting for her in the lounge. Nora is driving to Sunny's house to drop her off. All four people in the car are quiet, lost in their own thoughts. Lily seems excited about playing the online game. Nora keeps her eyes on the road as she drives. Sunny looks dismayed, thinking about what Grace said and wondering why she called her Julie. Elena sneaks a glance at the back of Sunny's head from the rear seat. She looks like she is pondering why Grace addressed Sunny by the name "Julie." Grace mentioned Sunny twice as if she is sure Sunny must be Julie. Elena shakes her head, doubting that Sunny is Julie, her late biological mother. She sighs and says to herself, "It can't be."

At that moment, "What? Did you say something to me?" Lily says, looking at Elena.

"No. I'm gonna tell you later."

That night, at Sunny's house, Sunny can't stop thinking about what Grace said. As far as she knew, Grace didn't show any sign of insanity though she was weak after skipping meals several days. She is absolutely certain that Grace wasn't out of her mind. As a mother of two sons, Sunny could ignore what Grace said, but oddly enough she can't let it go from her mind. In fact, she can't remember how she lived before waking up in the hospital, where Alex saved her.

When Alex sits next to her after dinner, Sunny brings up the past.

"Alex, about fourteen years ago when you saved me, did I tell you my name?"

"No, you didn't say a word after you awoke from a faint. Looking back, I was shocked when I found you were leaning against my car, unconscious. Right away, I put you in the car and drove to the nearest hospital. Luckily, you were okay but speechless. So I named you Sunny, my then-deceased wife. After recovery, I found out you were educated as a lawyer. But you didn't know your name or workplace. You didn't remember anything about yourself. So, I applied for a new

ID for you and took you and Mike to the States to live."

"Yeah, it's an old story. You saved me! What if my name was Julie?" Sunny says, looking at Alex.

"Was there anyone who said that name?" Alex asks with his eyes wide open.

Sunny explains what happened in the afternoon with Grace at the nursing home.

"Really? You mean, with Elena's grandma. By the way, you still don't remember anything about yourself, do you?" Alex asks.

Sunny shakes her head, frustrated by her amnesia that makes it difficult for her to recall any detail of her life before she was found by Alex.

"Honey, forget it. And you'd better not go to that place. If you are bored, you can take some classes at the cultural center." Alex says and puts his arm around her shoulder.

Sunny rests her head on his chest, feeling comfortable.

Two years have passed since Elena began to live at Nora's condo. Meanwhile, Lily has transferred to a local high school, and so, Lily and Elena go to the same school. In that March, they both begin studies at the same college and enjoy the campus. And Mike is busy with the process of applying to colleges in the US.

Elena works a part-time job to pay Nora for her living costs though she receives an allowance from Grace. Nora declines her payment though Elena insists on paying for the meal. Elena also visits Grace as often as she can. Grace is happier than ever before because she has her granddaughter by her side. So, she knows what more she can ask for, accepting the fact that her own son, Henry, has been like a stranger for nearly two decades.

One Sunday afternoon in April, Elena gets a phone call when she is enjoying her free time with Mike and Lily at the indoor climbing gym.

"Hi, Grandma. What's up?"

Elena hears Grace sobbing over the phone. Elena startles and asks, "Grandma! What's happening?"

"Your mom's here! Julie is here in front of me!"

"What? What are you talking about? Grandma! I'm on my way." Elena yells at Grace and goes to the locker to change her clothes. Mike and Lily follow her without asking why.

On the bus ride to the nursing home, Elena explains what she heard from Grace in a trembling voice.

Elena quickly enters Grace's room and stands frozen like a statue when she sees Sunny sitting by Grace's bed.

"Oh, Mrs. Hong?" Elena doubts her eyes.

Immediately, Grace exclaims, "Yes, Sunny is actually Julie! I was right!"

Sunny watches Elena, shedding tears.

At that moment, Mike and Lily come in the room.

Mike seems astonished, "Mom! Why are you here?"

Without answering Mike, Sunny pulls Elena to her side and holds her tight. Elena is just standing, speechless.

"Sweetie, my daughter, I had amnesia and I couldn't remember anything before I met Alex. I'm so sorry I couldn't recognize you," Sunny sobs, holding Elena's hands.

After gazing at Sunny for minutes, Elena says calmly, "Oh, Mrs. Hong... Mom... I finally meet you after seventeen years. I feel like I'm dreaming. By the way, how could you remember all this?"

"About two years ago I was curious about why Grace named me Julie. Since then, I have thought about that name. And then, suddenly, my memory came back with fragments of things. I was Julie and gave birth to you."

Mike cuts in the conversation, "So, Mom, you gave birth to Elena? Then, are Elena and I twin?"

"No, you both are not biologically related. Elena is your stepsister. There is one thing Alex and I didn't tell you."

Sunny takes a deep breath and continues, "Listen, Mike, you're a man, right? I believe you'll be fine if I tell you this. Your real mom passed away due to a disease when you were a baby, and I met Alex while suffering from amnesia. So, I couldn't remember having a baby daughter, or even my own name."

Mike is quiet for a second and then says, "I see. But you're my mom no matter what. You raised me with so much love and care."

And then, Lily looks at Elena and Mike in turn, and says, "Wow! What a surprise! You're stepsiblings!"

"Things happen!"

Elena and Mike say, looking at Sunny with a bashful look. Sunny just smiles at them without saying a word. Instead, she turns her head to Grace and says, "Mother, I can't believe this moment is happening!"

Grace nods and says with emotion, "Yes, it's happening in my life."

As Grace listens to conversations in the room, she feels a sense of belonging and filled with joy for having Julie back. Sometime later, Sunny gently pulls Elena and Mike over to the side of Grace's bed to take a picture. Four of them beam big smiles toward the cell phone. Grace seems to be at the happiest point in her life.

The April sun shines brightly outside the window of Grace's room.

초판 1쇄 발행일 | 2025년 3월 7일
지은이 | 김학진
펴낸이 | 김동명
펴낸곳 | 도서출판 창조와 지식
디자인 | 주식회사 북모아
인쇄처 | 주식회사 북모아
출판등록번호 | 제2018-000027호
주소 | 서울특별시 강북구 덕릉로 144
전화 | 1644-1814
팩스 | 02-2275-8577

ISBN 979-11-6003-772-2 (03840)

값 10,000원

이 책은 저작권법에 따라 보호받는 저작물이므로 무단 전재와 무단 복제를 금지하며,
이 책 내용을 이용하려면 반드시 저작권자와 도서출판 창조와 지식의 서면동의를 받아야 합니다.
잘못된 책은 구입처나 본사에서 바꾸어 드립니다.

지식의 가치를 창조하는 도서출판 창조와 지식
www.mybookmake.com